IT'S NATI

MY BEARING WITNESS WRITTEN IN RHYME

DR. DYSON X SLATER

BREAD BOOKS LLC

Title: IT'S NATION TIME: MY BEARING WITNESS WRITTEN IN RHYME

Copyright © 2023 Dr. Dyson X Slater

All rights reserved.

No part of this publication may be reproduced, distributed, or transmitted in any form or by any means, including photocopying, recording, or other electronic or mechanical methods, without the prior written permission of the author, except in the case of brief quotations embodied in critical reviews and certain other noncommercial uses permitted by copyright law.

This book of poems is a work of fiction. Any references to historical events, real people, or real places are used fictitiously.

Print ISBN - 13: 9798393339326

Book Cover by: Renee Luke of Cover Me Book Cover

Printed in The United States of America

First Printed in 2023

DEDICATION

In The Name of Allah, The Beneficent, The Merciful.

I bear witness that there is no God but Allah, who came to US in the person of Master Fard Muhammad. I bear witness that the Most Honorable Elijah Muhammad is the Messenger of Allah and now Exalted Christ. Furthermore, I bear witness that the Honorable Minister Louis Farrakhan is Allah's Divine Reminder, Divine Guide, Divine Warner and Messiah in OUR midst.

As- Salaam Alaikum!

*****

Beloved Reader,

Through the grace of Allah, I completed this book today, June 6, 2022, as I entered my 29th year of physical imprisonment under the awesome weight of an unjust Death Sentence, and sunset was 9:07 PM this day - which numerically matches my September 7th (9-07) Birth Anniversary. With this book's completion, I now dedicate this book to ALL who have and are presently laboring to mentally resurrect the Black Man, Black Woman and Black Child of America and throughout the world. Moreover, this book is dedicated to ALL who have and are presently laboring to remove Satan and his band of Devils from the planet, so that WE may establish God's Kingdom of Freedom, Justice, Equality and Islam (submission to God's will) throughout the world. May Master Fard Muhammad receive my prayer and grant the Righteous by Nature success.

As - Salaam Alaikum!

I Am,
Dyson X

CONTENTS

Title Page	1
Copyright	2
Dedication	3
Introduction	9
This Is My Prayer (Part I)	11
It's Nation Time	12
Dear Master Fard Muhammad	13
NOI Brotherhood	14
The Minister's Instruction	15
Baby Language Exit	16
F.A.I.T.H.	17
F.R.U.I.T.	18
Who Is My Best Friend	19
The	20
Fun-Learning Sensation	21
W.I.F.E.	22
H.U.S.B.A.N.D.	23
Missive To Elijah	24
Dyson's Angels	25

Mea Culpa	26
Attention!!	27
Bismillah	28
My Prayer Rug	29
Self Creation OUR Example	30
The Original Nigger	31
Submissions Consequence	32
Unlimited Necessary One	33
Justice … Or Else! (10-10-15)	34
Who Is The Original Man	35
Letter To The Honorable Minister Louis Farrakhan	36
Accept Your Own And Be Yourself	38
Soar	39
MGT	40
Thanksgiving	41
Meet The Hypocrites	42
F.O.I.	44
When Is Failure Always Impossible	46
A Good Name Is Better Than Gold	47
D.R.E.A.M.	49

A.T.O.M.I.C.	50
Black People	51
Value The Black Woman Pledge	52
The Black Man Anthem	54
This Is My Prayer (Part II)	57
Acknowledgements	59
About The Author	61

INTRODUCTION

Why Forty Entries In this Book?

The Most Honorable Elijah Muhammad teaches US that life begins at age forty!

Therefore, I thought it fitting to place forty entries into this book wherein I am bearing witness to the global necessity of the *life-giving*, *saving* and *improving* teachings of the Most Honorable Elijah Muhammad as represented to US today by the Honorable Minister Louis Farrakhan.

These forty entries represent how The Supreme Wisdom given to US by Master Fard Muhammad via the Most Honorable Elijah Muhammad and the Honorable Minister Louis Farrakhan marks the beginning of my life on ALL levels the moment I submitted and became a student of this "Trinity of Divinity".

This Is My Prayer (Part I)

Dear Lord, this is my prayer
To enrich the lives of others
To see the whole human family
As my beloved sisters and brothers
Equip me to lead OUR babies
On a path that never falters
Please use me to lift up
ALL OUR fallen sons and daughters
Help me to help the helpless
When no one else ever bothers
Make me the answer to prayers
Of OUR enslaved Mothers and Fathers

Amen.

It's Nation Time

What time is it
It's Nation Time
My bearing witness
Written in rhyme

I discovered Allah
Once I was jailed
For Islam came
Once ALL else failed

Violent prison yard
A cold stoned cell
Sentenced to death
My own living hell

In triple darkness
Hope's out of sight
I drop to my knees
Seeking God's light

At my lowest point
Farrakhan saved me
By introducing Elijah
W.D. Fard set me free

Morning prayer time
The call is the Adhan
After my Fajr prayer
I study my Holy Qur'an

With Self Knowledge
I walk this new path
Righteous my nature
My theology is math

Studying my lessons
To memory I commit
I recite every word
So I'll never forget

Supreme the Wisdom
Actual ALL the Facts
Restrictive the Laws
Salvation for Blacks

On September seventh
In year of the Lord "95"
I enrolled in my Nation
That's when I came alive

In charge of my post
Active Fruit of Islam
It's an FOI life for me
No more living haram

Asking what is a Fruit
Say a Fruit is the Best
Trained & conditioned
To overcome every test

Equalling myself to God
Jesus said wasn't a crime
So for the rest of my life
I'll declare It's Nation Time

Dear Master Fard Muhammad

God, You've done so much for me
To address You, where do I begin
Asking how do I thank You, Allah
For fishing me from a sea of sin

Minister Farrakhan drew me in
Elijah Muhammad cast the rod
Your servants resurrected me
Now I've fully submitted to God

Fard, I Love You with ALL my soul
So my heart's ALL Yours, it's true
I'll serve You the rest of my life
That'll be how I'll say thank You

NOI Brotherhood

WE soldier together for Allah's cause
Desiring for each other only good
You've passed from death to life
When you Love the brotherhood

The Minister's Instruction

I can't live without the truth
Now this is my life's hallmark
These words I live my life by
Farrakhan ignited this spark

I obey the Jesus in OUR midst
He's the Messiah of the hour
An extension of Allah's Love
Backed by the Mahdi's Power

His every word my command
It's his guidance I will follow
Receiver of revelation today
Saving US now and tomorrow

Baby Language Exit

Now here's what they say
Water seeks its own level
It's language of The Gods
Or the babble of the devil

Actual when I was a child
Factual I spoke as a child
My speech was immature
Full of stupidity and wild

But when I became a man
Adult became my speech
The student of a Master
Who exalted me to teach

Freedom Justice Equality
From my mouth now pour
A Supreme Wisdom orator
Baby language is no more

F.A.I.T.H.

Following Allah Into The Hereafter

F.R.U.I.T.

Fearless Rulers United In Truth

WHO IS MY BEST FRIEND

IS IT HIM
IS IT HER
WHO COULD IT BE

ALLAH HAS SHOWN
IT IS HE
THAT RESIDES IN ME

THE

ELITE MATHEMATICIAN
CEREBRAL PHYSICIAN
PSYCHOLOGICAL TECHNICIAN
LINGUISTIC MAGICIAN

THEOLOGICAL ORATOR
UNIVERSAL CREATOR
IMMORTAL JUDICATOR
MORAL LEGISLATOR

SPIRITUALLY PROFOUND
POLITICALLY UNBOUND
DIVINELY FOUND
INTELLECTUALLY SOUND

RIGHTEOUS MOTIVATOR
INSPIRED CALCULATOR
ESOTERIC REVELATOR
GALACTIC DICTATOR

SUPREME BEING
SLAVE FREEING
ALL EYE SEEING
APOSTLE FEEING

HUMANITY BENEFACTOR
BLESSING TRANSACTOR
ETERNAL PROTRACTOR
CELESTIAL EXACTOR

Fun-Learning Sensation

What is fun to Allah
The answer learning
To gain more wisdom
A perpetual yearning

Unlocking the mystic
Or Universal mystery
Allah in Master Fard
He possesses the key

Executing divine force
Executing divine power
WE follow His example
So WE grow every hour

None are more zealous
In pursuing knowledge
The students of Elijah
Are in the Best college

Now pardon my French
Not college University
Justifying OUR existence
Makes US equal and free

So Elijah's best student
Is OUR studious paragon
Now who is this student
It is Minister Farrakhan

For Black People to rise
Knowledge of Self is key
In order to crack open
The God in you and me

So a day does not expire
Wherein WE don't learn
OUR fire to know more
Shall perennially burn

Universal is the lessons
The Stars Moon and Sun
Like the Creator of US ALL
WE know learning as fun

W.I.F.E.

Wonderfully Intelligent Female Entity

Proverbs 18:22   Proverbs 19:14

H.U.S.B.A.N.D.

Handsome Universal Supreme Being Adding New Dimensions

I Corinthians 7:3   I Corinthians 7:4

Missive To Elijah

Dear Honorable Elijah Muhammad
Though small in weight and height
You're large where it counts most
By way of submission to Fard's light

Allah came in the Person of a Man
3 ½ years taught you day and night
Then left you with a heavy mission
To raise and lead your people right

For Supreme Wisdom, WE thank you
Resurrecting US with divine insight
With Satan battling to take US down
You taught US how to win this fight

The Nation of Islam is a solid wall
Love of self keeps OUR ranks tight
As your faith in Allah protected you
We're also trusting in Allah's might

Thank you for your sacrifices Elijah
Thank you for giving OUR people sight
ALL Black people owe you great honor
So does all humanity, including whites

On a personal note, I thank you, Elijah
For your saving me from Satan's bite
With knowledge of self you saved me
I no longer suffer from mental blight

Exalted Christ, my life I owe to you
ALL you've done for me, I don't take lite
It's my gratitude and love for you
That's motivated these words I write

Dyson's Angels

I have a circle of Angels
That surround me with Love
They are not of this world
These Angels are sent from above

Coming in ALL shapes and sizes
These Angels are tailored to me
Whenever I need some help
They're the only ones I see

When it's storming in my life
They cover me with Angelic Wings
When I see only evil ahead
They guide me to good things

Angels coming in ALL different colors
Blending easily into any background
They sneak up on my enemies
Without ever making a sound

I have my own Angelic Army
Eliminating every one of my foes
Every time my mind is troubled
They relieve ALL my woes

I know I'm under Divine favor
And thankful for my Angelic host
I Love ALL of my Angels
But I Love Allah the most

For without you, my Dear Lord
My band of Angels wouldn't be
Lord, please look after the Angels
That are always looking after me

Mea Culpa

Ash and sackcloth
My humble attire
Need of forgiveness
My earnest desire

I now prostrate
Most submissive position
Atoning for sin
Immersed in contrition

Heal my wronged
Let them rise
From my heart
I sincerely apologize

ATTENTION!!

ORIGINAL SALUTE
READY FRONT
CADENCE CRISP
COMMAND BLUNT

ABOUT FACE
SECURITY ACHIEVED
I'LL STAY ON MY POST
UNTIL PROPERLY RELIEVED

Bismillah

In The Name of Allah
Everything WE think
Everything WE say
Everything WE do

In The Name of Allah
The Creator of ALL
The Creator of me
The Creator of you

In The Name of Allah
WE begin OUR every day
WE end OUR every night
WE wake again to renew

In The Name of Allah
Labor's the Original Muslim
Labor's the Original Christian
Labor's the Original Hebrew

In The Name of Allah
From dawn beyond sunlight
From beginning with no end
From an Atom of Life ALL grew

In The Name of Allah
In the sea the fish swam
In the land the beast ran
In the air the birds flew

In The Name of Allah
WE find out life's aim
WE find out who WE are
WE find out ALL that's true

In The Name of Allah
The Righteous prosper
The Righteous rejoice
The Righteous bid sin ado

My Prayer Rug

Where I'm most at peace
Where I feel most divine
The source of this calm
This prayer rug of mine

Cleanse my entire body
Pure mind, body, and soul
To commune with Allah
My primary desired goal

I say Allah's the Greatest
My hands up in surrender
Standing upright for now
I seek Allah as my Defender

I say Allah's the Greatest
I Am bent hands to knees
My supplication to Allah
Use me as You will please

I say Allah's the Greatest
Now down on ALL four
My forehead's to the rug
Allah, improve me I implore

I say Allah's the Greatest
On my knees upright I sit
I declare to the Most High
From my sinful life I quit

Peace and Mercy of Allah
Right to left be unto you
Subsequently I say Ameen
Now my prayer is through

Rolling up my prayer rug
Now I'm feeling so pristine
Fueled for service to Allah
Thru me may His will be seen

Self Creation OUR Example

In triple darkness
Temperature so cold
Six trillion years
Without any ally
Not a problem
He embraced Himself
Light of Himself
Certain His thoughts
Determined the idea
Unwavering the vision
Indomitable His will
Singular the focus
Goal concentrated I
Not a distraction
Benefit of isolation
ALL foes vanquished
Victorious this Warrior
Destroyed the impossible
Follow His example
Celebrate your alone
Unite with Essence
Made up mind
The Greatest Force
Overcome ALL difficulties
Allah and you
Make the majority
Do ALL things
When by yourself
Begin Self Creating

The Original Nigger

The pale skinned troglodyte
Walking on all fours
A dog's best friend
Prisoner of European tours

History written in blood
Skunk of the Planet Earth
The Brown Germ manifest
Mischief-maker since birth

German Shepherd hair shedding
The author of cremation
This poison animal eater
Enslaver of the Black Nation

Supplanter of the Righteous
Open enemy of truth
Diametrically opposed to Allah
Originator of the K-9 tooth

Carrier of all disease
Satan with blue eyes
Hell on two legs
Reason the world cries

Lover of raw flesh
Savage to the core
The alpha sexual deviant
The first recorded whore

It's Yacub's Grafted Devil
The Master of Disaster
The interpolation of scripture
The genesis christian pastor

The 6000-year ruler
Preacher of "God's unseen"
The father of lies
Reign ending in 1914

Grafted brains six ouncer
The existing recessive race
Corruptor of the planet
The White Supremacist face

2000 year cave inmate
Weak bone, blood, and flesh
Advocate for the stale
Adversary of the fresh

Thin nose and lips
Object of a nefarious file
The ultimate covenant breaker
Wearer of a crooked smile

This wicked universal Snooper
This criminal grave digger
Native nowhere on Earth
It's the Original Nigger

Submissions Consequence

Luxury
Money
Good homes
Friendships in ALL walks of life

Righteous
Is the circle
Righteous
The husband and wife

Lifting
Fallen humanity
Resurrecting
The mentally dead

The last
Has become first
The tails
Become the head

First seek
The Kingdom of heaven
And ALL
Of its righteousness

Then Allah
In Fard's person
Will grant you that
And he'll give you this

Unlimited Necessary One

Can One
Having One heart
Love more than One

Does not One sun
Having One constant light
Shine on more than One

Is not One Love
Like the One sun
Needed by everyone

One "Yes"
The One answer
For ALL the above Ones

Justice . . . Or Else! (10-10-15)

400 plus years is long enough
ALL cowards get out of the way
If you sympathize with the enemy
You can die with them today

WE will just take OUR reparations
No more will you deprive US
Your oppression of US is over
You have served US enough injustice

Minister Farrakhan has given the call
In Allah's name WE ALL come
No smiles are on OUR faces
WE are beating the war drum

The command is "Justice . . . Or Else!"
There's nothing more to be said
The enemy better give US "Justice"
"Or Else!" it's off with their head

Who Is The Original Man

The Asiatic Black Man
The Father of Civilization
The First of ALL Beings
The Source of ALL Creation

He Is The Maker
The Colored Man Producer
The 600-Year Grafter
The Wicked-Race Reducer

He Is The Owner
THe Real Estate Inventor
The King Over ALL
The Only True Center

The Cream of The Planet Earth
The Almighty Life Writer
The Upholder of Existence
The Righteous Cause Fighter

The God of The Universe
The Greatest of the Great
The Author of The Worlds
The Living God Without Debate

Letter To The Honorable Minister Louis Farrakhan

Dear Honorable Minister Louis Farrakhan
May this letter find you in wonderful health
May Allah continue to impregnate you
With His spirit and the truest wealth

Beloved, I have composed this letter
To let you know how much you mean to me
It is because of you, my dear leader
That I know what it is to be truly free

It is because of Allah I have been found
It is because of Satan I was once lost
Allah brought you into my life as a Saviour
To redeem me, you've paid the ultimate cost

I will thank Allah for May 11, 1933 forever
For that is when WE were blessed with your presence
Since 1995, I have studied you with meticulous care
Desiring to gain a double portion of your essence

I thank the Most Honorable Elijah Muhammad
For leaving US with a comforter that is you
Master Fard Muhammad has exalted Elijah
And now you are guided by the Great Two

Letter To The Honorable Minister Louis Farrakhan (Continued)

Since you were given as a Saviours' Day gift
You have served OUR Nation beginning in 1955
You have been a faithful warner to US ALL
While declaring that Elijah is alive

Under your divine tutelage, I became a man
The knowledge of self, I practice every day
I wanted to set myself in heaven at once
And, Minister, you have shown me the way

You have made me a soldier for Muhammad
I will always fight for Freedom, Justice, and Equality
You taught me that Islam is my nature
And then you connected me to the God in me

A loyal servant to OUR people, you've made of me
Never again by OUR open enemy will I be conned
I thank you for sacrificing your life for me
And straight from my heart, I love you, Farrakhan

Accept Your Own And Be Yourself

WE must do for Self
Or suffer the consequence
The choice is easy
No need for hesitance

WE share the same struggle
WE share the same enemy
They want to destroy you
They want to destroy me

You and I are targets
Of an evilly-styled plan
Born in the wicked mind
Of the satanic colored man

If WE would only unite
WE would find OUR power
That will get US through
This most perilous hour

WE are invincible
As a collective band
Witness the rise
Of the Original Man

Soar

Challenge yourself daily to be better
Write yourself an inspirational letter

No bird can fly as high as you
No great one can do what you do

ALL you want is within your grasp
ALL you need, you can certainly have

Up Up Up and Away you go
The world's a stage; it's your show

Say I will always be a friend to *me*
Say I will never be my own enemy

Look in the mirror; you see greatness
Gravity has no effect; you're weightless

Work with faith; you'll have the best
Trust in the Lord; He'll do the rest

The winner's announced; you stand alone
It's divinely ordained; inherit your throne

Sow seeds of Love; reap success as your fruit
You can do all things when God's at the root

MGT

She is the epitome
Of Allah's ideology
Of what true beauty
Was created to be

The model of
Second act of creativity
But equal in divinity
While first in quality

Guardian of God's mystery
Sacred Womb of nativity
Mother of ALL humanity
The child's first university

From Allah's own anatomy
He fashioned her biology
Serving as his serenity
After His war activity

The paragon of dignity
Matriculated in the GCC
Now introducing to thee
The highly honored MGT

Thanksgiving

Daily, ALL praises are due to The One that created…

. . . These hands to labor for Him and lift fallen humanity upright that WE may be what He created US to "BE", i.e., perfect reflections of Him.

. . . These feet to walk up and down in the Earth seeking whom I may empower in His Name while establishing His Kingdom wherever I travel.

. . . These eyes to see the Light of His Majesty that I may use it as a torch to illuminate the path that leads to salvation for those who now walk in gross darkness.

. . . These ears to receive His message and hear the cries of the suffering masses that are in dire need of the Life-giving and saving truth He invested in me.

. . . These lips to preach glad tidings to ALL and to speak on behalf of the voiceless and downtrodden whom He has come to save.

. . . These gifts, talents, and skills to be used in service to Him alone on behalf of His creation for the rest of my life and beyond.

Happy Thanksgiving!

Meet the Hypocrites

As-Salaam Alaikum is the cloak
Plotting your demise is the dagger
Watch them parade into the mosque
In unison with a deceitful swagger

On his shoulders sits a head
Double the size of Mr. Yacub
Sitting at the table with believers
Pretending to be a believer too

She is dressed head to toe
In the finest of Muslim garb
On the outside appearing so devout
For an actress, that's not hard

He eats away at the brotherhood
Like a wooden cabin to termites
She sucks away at the sisterhood
Like an open wound to parasites

A greater dancer than 100 disbelievers
Is just one of these saboteurs
Because they poison the believing body
For them, there are no cures

Meet the Hypocrites
(Continued)

You must surgically remove this disease
Only Allah can make this incision
With His word as your scalpel
They will be extracted with precision

They promise to you one thing
But their word is not bond
Their word's contrary to their heart
As written in the Holy Qur'an

They desire to steal your joy
Weak Muslims fall for their con
They solicit the righteous like prostitutes
Knowing that a "trick" is a john

My warning to the Muslim family
Be on the watch for hypocrites
And take solace in the fact
Their final stop is the abyss

F.O.I.

Crafted from the best mold
Built strong, Black, and bold
Under pressure, will never fold
Making sure truth is told

Showing Fruit is the Best
Always ready for every test
Moving only at Allah's behest
Laboring on a righteous quest

Proving God's the Black Man
Never saying "can't" only "can"
Fulfillers of a divine plan
From the enemy, never ran

The Image of the Lord
The Actual Facts OUR sword
Pushing devils off the board
Heaven on Earth striving toward

F.O.I.
(Continued)

Final call pushing to proselytize
The noble goal to civilize
Returning sight to blind eyes
In God's likeness, WE materialize

For Elijah Muhammad, WE stand
Giving Minister Farrakhan a hand
We're Master Fard Muhammad's band
Removing Satan from every land

The Original Man is here
Facing danger with no fear
Making Allah's word crystal clear
Saviors in God's military gear

WE only "do" never "try"
Back up forty miles high
Well made men that fly
WE are the "Mighty" F.O.I.

When Is Failure Always Impossible

When your whole lifestyle is righteous
When buried under dirt, mud and sod
You will never be denied true success
When you're on a mission from God

When your faith can never be destroyed
You patiently endure strokes from His rod
Your faithful service is always rewarded
When you're on a mission from God

When you accept the difficult walk with Him
Over the easier swim with the evil pod
I assure that failure is always impossible
When you're on a mission from God

A Good Name Is Better Than Gold

For years, I was proud
Of my last name Slater
Until learning it's the name
Of a slave master and trader
Who made my greatest grandfather work
From dawn 'til sun out of sight
Then go to the slave quarters
To rape my greatest grandmother at night
He forced my ancestors to labor
Until their entire bodies ached
And this sadistic slave driver
Refused to give my people a break
He whipped them without mercy
And commanded them back to work
Then savagely beat them some more
For getting negro blood on his shirt
The so-called food my people ate
Wasn't considered fit for a dog
Cornbread, greens, black eyed peas
And the body of that filthy old hog

A Good Name Is Better Than Gold (Continued)

To be a slave was a horrible life
And my people hated the slave trader
Who stripped from them everything
And forced upon them the name Slater
So I'll never wear the name Slater
In honor of my enslaved ancestors
Who despised the slave name Slater
From the "S" down to the last letter
That's why I now wear the "X"
In place of that former last name
Because I don't know my true title
And ALL participants in slavery, I blame
But I'll tell you forthright
My wonderful friend
My name is not Slater
And don't call me that again
I thank you so much
For showing me respect
And when you greet me from now on
Say As-Salaam Alaikum Dyson X

D.R.E.A.M.

Desires Realized Equals Action Manifested

A.T.O.M.I.C.

Allah's The Original Man's Internal Center

Black People

I have always Loved you
I just didn't know how
Seeking how to Love you
Before God, I had to bow

In answer of my prayer
Farrakhan came along
Teaching me Real Love
Before the Swan Song

Learning at his feet
Student of the divine
I learned how to Love
By renewal of my mind

Now I'm truly equipped
To serve is Love, I Know
My Love's beyond word
In action, now I'll show

Black People, here I Am
Serving day and night
For Allah's shown me
How to love you right

Value The Black Woman Pledge

I will value the Black woman
You will value the Black Woman
WE will value the Black Woman
ALL will value the Black Woman

Why?

Because,

Without her, there is no You
Without her, there is no Me
Through her womb, God escapes death
Through her, came everyone WE see

She is the co-creator with God
She is the Heaven here on Earth
She is the measure of ALL beauty
How can WE calculate her worth

Within her, WE find God's secret
Within her, WE find OUR origin
Know that she's OUR Mother Nature
Know that she's where WE begin

Her value is above the universe
Her value is more than ALL
Because of her, WE always win
Because of her, WE never fall

Value The Black Woman Pledge (Continued)

WE will make sure she is honored
WE will make sure she is respected
Black Man, always lift her up
Black Man, keep her forever protected

She is the child's first nurse
She is the child's first teacher
WE look to her for healing
WE look to her for a preacher

She is the Global Divine Queen
She is the Mother of civilization
In her, WE find OUR paradise
In her, WE find OUR salvation

I will value the Black Woman
You will value the Black Woman
WE will value the Black Woman
ALL will value the Black Woman

Why?

Because she's worth it and more

The Black Man Anthem

No right hand over the heart
Still, you'll feel Me the same
I have no beginning nor ending
And the Black Man's my name

I Am the Father of Civilization
Yes ALL people came through Me
I created myself from nothing
Including everything that you see

No right hand over the heart
Still, you'll feel me the same
I have no beginning nor ending
And the Black Man's my name

I Am the standard for ALL
Study me in the Holy Qur'an
I first called you to prayer
As the Creator of the Adhan

No right hand over the heart
Still, you'll feel me the same
I have no beginning nor ending
And the Black Man's my name

I Am the One Living God
There is none that can compare
The Universe submits to my will
As commands from my voice blare

The Black Man Anthem
(Continued)

No right hand over the heart
Still, you'll feel me the same
I have no beginning nor ending
And the Black Man's my name

I Am the kinetic energy displayer
Bringing ALL the hidden into view
I taught you red represents freedom
And deceit is represented by blue

No right hand over the heart
Still, you'll feel me the same
I have no beginning nor ending
And the Black Man's my name

I am the Omniscient Sovereign
Called the Best Knower by most
My Supreme Wisdom rules over ALL
As I lead my heavenly host

No right hand over the heart
Still, you'll feel me the same
I have no beginning nor ending
And the Black Man's my name

The Black Man Anthem
(Continued)

I Am the bestower of blessings
The dutiful provider of my family
I protect my woman and child
The real Black Man is Me

No right hand over the heart
Still, you'll feel me the same
I have no beginning nor ending
And the Black Man's my name

No right hand over the heart
Still, you'll feel me the same
I have no beginning nor ending
And the Black Man's my name

No right hand over the heart
Still, you'll feel me the same
I have no beginning nor ending
And the Black Man's my name

This Is My Prayer (Part II)

*Dear Lord, this is my prayer
To be better than good
To serve You and Your creation
The way I know I should
When others foolishly choose Satan
It is with You, I've stood
You led me out of darkness
Like I knew that You would
You cleaned up my corrupt mind
The masterful way only You could
Thank You for sparing my life
I didn't die in the "hood"*

Amen

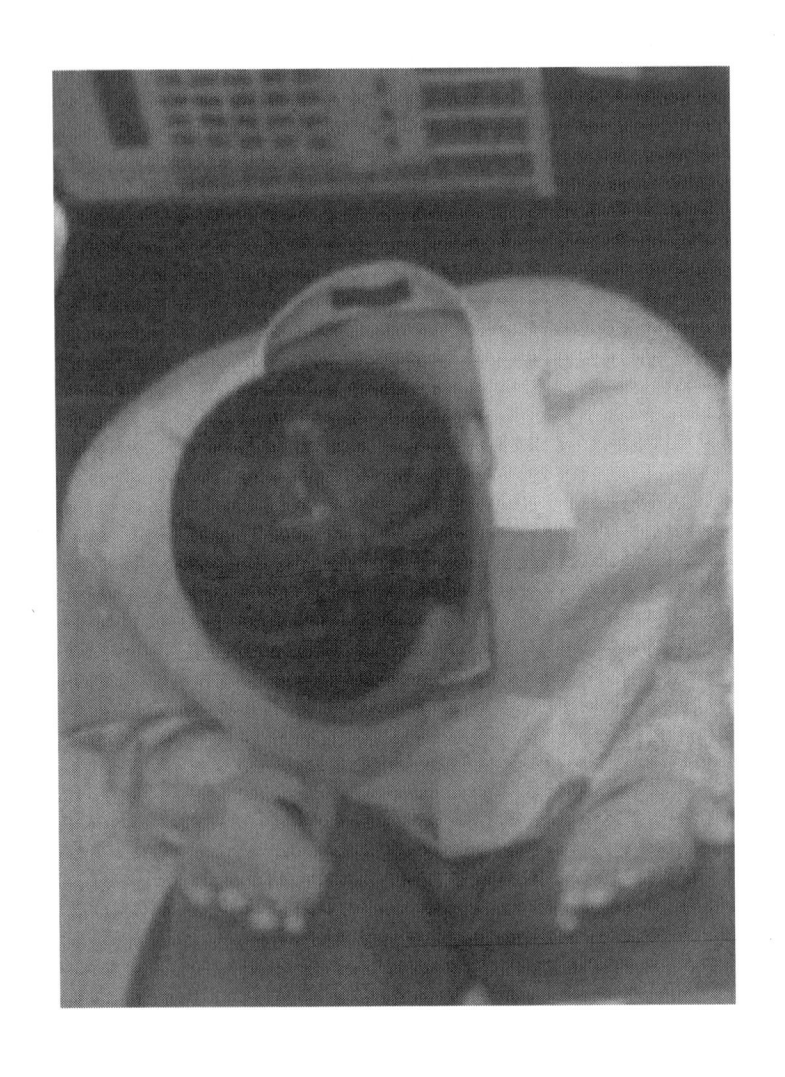

Dr. Dyson X Slater

"And your Lord says: Pray to Me, I will answer you."

Holy Quran 40:60

ACKNOWLEDGEMENTS

SPECIAL THANKS ROLL CALL

Special thanks to Nation of Islam Student National Prison Reform Minister Abduallah Muhammad and all those within the NOI Prison Reform Ministry, especially my brother and friend Student Minister Karl 3X Little.

Special thanks to my beloved niece, Tiyia James – my typist extraordinaire. You truly are a godsend and the gift that keeps on giving in my life.

Special thanks to my dearly loved mother, Mrs. Eileen Slater-Hinton, A.K.A. "Scoop", for the labor of love you performed on my behalf to bring this book into existence. Thank you for all of your sacrifices to make my desire a reality. You are my maternal angel, and I find solace under your wings.

I love all of you, and may Allah in the person of Master Fard Muhammad continue to bless all of you for continuing to be a blessing to me and innumerable others.

ABOUT THE AUTHOR

Dyson Slater was born and raised in Ypsilanti, Michigan. In 1990 he graduated from Ypsilanti High School, and as one that has always hungered and thirsted for knowledge, he went on to attend Ferris State University (Big Rapids, Michigan) and DeVry Technical Institute (Columbus, Ohio). In 1994, Brother Dyson's pursuit of higher education was derailed by his illicit lifestyle that landed him in prison. While in prison, Brother Dyson dedicated himself to self-improvement in every area of his life; and to achieve this noble goal, he enrolled into Muhammad's Islamic University wherein he's majoring in "The Knowledge of Self".

Heretofore, Brother Dyson has become A Certified Ordained Minister; A Certified Doctor of Divinity; A Certified Counselor in "The Science of Universal Life"; A Certified Counselor in the areas of "Conflict Resolution", "Parenting" and "Substance Abuse"; A Certified Paralegal; A Certified Specialist in Fitness Nutrition; A Certified Travel Agent; Certified in Business Education Training; and a recipient of numerous certificates and awards for the positive example and works he's performed inside and outside of prison.

Brother Dyson finds great pleasure in authoring books, stage plays, and songs. He is also currently creating a movie script based on his journey of atonement, redemption, and reconciliation. Lastly, Brother Dyson's greatest pleasure is in serving Allah (God), all of His creation, and working to establish Freedom, Justice, and Equality for all.

Made in the USA
Columbia, SC
09 June 2023